Down at The Seaweed Café

story by Robert Perry

illustrations by **Greta Guzek**

NIGHTWOOD EDITIONS

Everyone's welcome
At The Seaweed Café,
Where seaweed tea
Is served all day,

Where you may hear
Some salty tales,
Or watch for ships
Or seals or whales.

"Come right on in,
I'll show you round:
Tables and chairs
From driftwood we've found;

Lamps from bottles
Washed in on the tide;
Bowls from shells;
Seaweed we've dried.

Have a sip
Of seaweed tea,
In a bull-kelp cup—
Ah, the taste of the sea!

Menu

Seaweed Tea

Tsunami Blend | 10c
Moonlight Blend | 10c

Snacks

Seaweed wrap | 10c
Seaweed salad | 10c
blackberry dream | 10c

Or crunchy snacks
Fresh from the shore
Where seaweeds grow
And breakers roar.

Here you may watch
The boats go by
And flocks of birds
Circle the sky.

Keep an eye
On seagull Sly —
Hc'll snatch your food
And off he'll fly!

The regulars
Are wandering in,
And storytelling
Will soon begin.

Now who can tell
The tallest tale
Of things that swim
Or things that sail?"

"From beach to beach
     I've roamed and roamed,
In search of treasure
I've combed and combed.

One day I found
A Spanish wreck
With bags of gold
Below the deck!"

"The whales were here,
The whales were there,
The whales were jumping
Everywhere!

When out of the blue
One raised my boat,
I found myself
No longer afloat!"

"For years and years
      I kept the light,
         Watched it go round
         And round at night —

But nothing ever
Matched the sight
Of Cadborosaurus
In all his might!"

"While I sat on
The wharf one day,
A giant fish
Swam into the bay —

But looking closer —
You'll think I'm a fool –
That giant fish
Had gone to school!"

"Far, far away,
   A wave began
      The journey from
         The shores of Japan;

So high it rose
　　Above the seas,
　　　It left some fish
　　　　Up in our trees!"

"Thank you, thank you,
One and all;
Every tale
Was truly tall.

Who loves to sing?
Who loves to dance?
Let's move the tables!
Let's light the lamps!"

One plays a flute,
One plays a drum,
One plays a fiddle,
While others hum.

Then in a swirl,
A swaying trance,
A few begin
The seaweed dance.

Above the foam
On ocean trail,
A pod of whales
Is setting sail.

Across the deck
In the setting sun,
Some playful otters
Quickly run.

The sky is now
A starlit dome;
The boats are all
Parading home.

The moon is bright,
The night is long,
So all join in
This salty song:

" Everyone's welcome
At The Seaweed Café,
Where seaweed tea
Is served all day,

Where you may hear
Some salty tales,
Or watch for ships
Or seals or whales."

First paperback edition published in 2010 by Nightwood Editions
3 4 5 6 — 20 19 18 17

Nightwood Editions
P.O. Box 1779
Gibsons, BC, V0N 1V0
Canada
www.nightwoodeditions.com

Edited by Simone Doust
Design by Ingrid Paulson
Printed and bound in China
Manufactured by Prolong Press Ltd, China, April 2017, Job #3654/6065

Nightwood Editions acknowledges financial support from the Government of Canada
through the Book Publishing Industry Development Program and the Canada
Council for the Arts, and from the Province of British Columbia through the BC Arts
Council and the Book Publishing Tax Credit.

LIBRARY AND ARCHIVES CANADA CATALOGUING IN PUBLICATION

Perry, Robert Graham, 1951-
    Down at the Seaweed Café / story by Robert
Perry ; illustrations by Greta Guzek.

Reading grade level: 2-3.
Interest age level: 3-8.
ISBN 978-0-88971-246-1

    I. Guzek, Greta II. Title.

PS8581.E74935D68 2009   jC813'.54   C2009-907418-4